BLUEY

DADDY PUTDOWN

Mum's going to a baby shower tonight. But Bluey doesn't want her to go, because Mum won't be there to put them to bed.
"I'll still come in and give you a goodnight kiss," says Mum.
"But I won't *feel* it," pleads Bluey.
"Yes, you will!" says Mum.

Bingo asks who will put them to bed.
"Your dad," says Mum. "It's a daddy putdown!"

As soon as Mum leaves, Bluey misses her.
"How about we play a game to take your mind off it?"
suggests Dad.
"Let's play Follow the Leader!" yells Bingo.

Bluey, Bingo and Dad head inside to play the game.
"Right. I am your magnificent leader. And you have to follow me!
You kids got that?!" growls Dad, in his most leader-like voice.
"Yes, leader," chorus Bluey and Bingo.

"Follow, follow, follow the leader . . ."

The kids follow their magnificent leader . . .

but not for long!

"What?! You were supposed to be following me," shouts Dad. "Get back in line. Sitting around will not be tolerated."

The game starts again, but the magnificent leader loses his followers. He can't find them in the lounge room . . .

or in the kitchen . . .

or in the bathroom . . .

GRR. WHERE'S THAT GIGGLING COMING FROM?!

They're not even in the backyard.

Follow the Leader is fun, but Bluey still misses Mum.
She needs another game to distract her. Bingo suggests
Come Here and Go Away.
Dad starts pushing Bluey and Bingo on the swing.
"Come here," says Dad. "OK, so . . ."

The girls giggle as they swing away from him.

HEY!
COME HERE!

They have a lot of fun . . . but Bluey is still sad.
"The games only take my mind off missing Mum for a little while.
Please can you call her?" asks Bluey.

"OK. It's just that she was really looking forward to this baby shower," says Dad, as the phone rings. "I don't understand it. Why would you want to watch some stinky baby have a shower?"

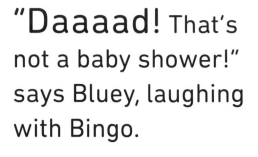

"Daaaad! That's not a baby shower!" says Bluey, laughing with Bingo.

Bluey and Bingo know that a baby shower is a party for someone who has a baby in their belly. This gives Bluey an idea for a game of her own. She races off! "Good work, Bluey," says Dad, hanging up the phone.

"Dad? How does the baby get into someone's belly?" asks Bingo.
Dad lets go of the swing.

Bluey pretends she's going to a baby shower. She has to leave her daughter, Snowdrop, with a babysitter. "No, Mama, no go. Me sad," says Snowdrop. She doesn't want her mum to leave, just like Bluey didn't.

Bluey is excited to see her friends. She has set up the baby shower, complete with decorations, snacks, games and presents. Oh, and one of Bluey's friends is pregnant, of course!

Bluey is having a great time at the baby shower. "I bet Mum is having a good time, too," says Bluey, opening a present.

Bluey likes dancing with her friends and eating cake. But her favourite game is trying to stick the dummy on the baby.

In the kitchen, Bingo and Dad are cooking dinner together.

They are peeling
the prawns . . .

stirring the rice . . .

and making a mess . . .

But daddy putdowns
are a lot of fun, too!

Bingo sets the table, and Dad carries over the hot food.

DINNER!

"Wow, it's dinnertime already," says Bluey. The afternoon
has gone by so quickly!
She waves goodbye and heads home so she can give
Snowdrop a goodnight kiss.

At dinner, Bluey tells Bingo and Dad all about the Baby Shower game. "There was even an obstacle course. It was so funny!" says Bluey.

The moon has risen, and the Heeler house is dark.
Except for the light left on in the front room for Mum.

Mum creeps in quietly and shuts the door behind her. She had a great time at the baby shower, but she can't wait to see how the daddy putdown has gone.

Mum checks on Bingo. She is sleeping soundly . . .

and so is Dad. Looks like the daddy putdown was a success.

Mum leans over and kisses Bluey goodnight.
And, even though Bluey is asleep, she can still feel it.

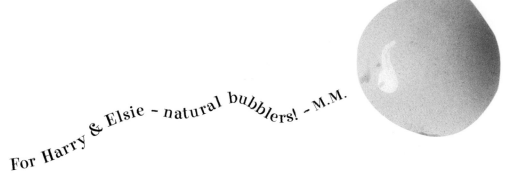

For Harry & Elsie - natural bubblers! - M.M.

For Holly, Craig & Marbles - P.D.

Quarto Knows

Inspiring | Educating | Creating | Entertaining

Brimming with creative inspiration, how-to projects, and useful information to enrich your everyday life, Quarto Knows is a favourite destination for those pursuing their interests and passions. Visit our site and dig deeper with our books into your area of interest: Quarto Creates, Quarto Cooks, Quarto Homes, Quarto Lives, Quarto Drives, Quarto Explores, Quarto Gifts, or Quarto Kids.

First published in 2008 by Frances Lincoln Children's Books.
This edition first published in 2020 by Frances Lincoln Children's Books,
an imprint of The Quarto Group.
The Old Brewery, 6 Blundell Street, London N7 9BH, United Kingdom.
T (0)20 7700 6700 F (0)20 7700 8066 www.QuartoKnows.com

ISBN 978-0-7112-5402-2

Set in Elroy

Manufactured in Guangdong, China TT012020

1 3 5 7 9 8 6 4 2

BUBBLE TROUBLE

Margaret Mahy

Polly Dunbar

Frances Lincoln
Children's Books

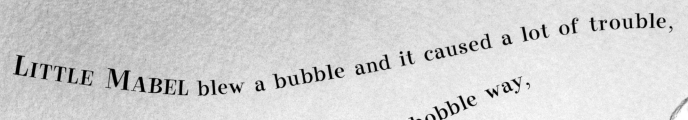

LITTLE MABEL blew a bubble and it caused a lot of trouble,

Such a lot of bubble trouble in a bibble-bobble way,

For it broke away from Mabel as it bobbed across the table,

Where it bobbled over Baby, and it wafted him away.

The baby didn't quibble. He began to smile and dribble,

For he liked the wibble-wobble of the bubble in the air.

But Mabel ran for cover as the bubble bobbed above her,

And she shouted out for Mother who was putting up her hair.

At the sudden cry of trouble, Mother took off at the double,
For the squealing left her reeling, made her terrified and tense,
Saw the bubble for a minute, with the baby bobbing in it,
As it bibbled by the letter-box and bobbed across the fence.

In her garden, Chrysta Gribble had begun to cry and cavil
At her lazy brother, Greville, reading novels in his bed.

But she bellowed,
"Gracious, Greville!"
and she grovelled on the gravel,

When the baby in the bubble
bibble-bobbled overhead.

In a garden folly, Tybal, and his jolly mother, Sybil,
Sat and played a game of Scrabble, shouting shrilly as they scored.
But they both began to babble and to scrobble with the Scrabble
As the baby in the bubble bibble-bobbled by the board.

Then crabby Mr Copple and his wife (a carping couple),
Set out arm in arm to hobble and to squabble down the lane.
But the baby in the bubble turned their hobble to a joggle
As they raced away like rockets – and they've never limped again.

Even feeble Mrs Threeble in a muddle with her needle
(Matching pink and purple patches for a pretty patchwork quilt)
When her older sister told her, tossed the quilt across her shoulder,
As she set off at a totter in her tattered tartan kilt.

At the shops a busy rabble met to gossip and to gabble,

Started gibbering and goggling as the bubble bobbled by.

Mother, hand in hand with Mabel, flew as fast as she was able,

Full of trouble lest the bubble burst or vanish in the sky.

After them came Greville Gribble in his nightshirt with his novel

(All about a haunted hovel) held up high above his head,

Followed by his sister, Chrysta (though her boots had made a blister),

Then came Tybal, pulling Sybil, with the Scrabble for a sled.

After them the Copple couple came cavorting at the double,

Then a jogger (quite a slogger) joined the crowd who called and coughed.

Up above the puzzled people - up towards the chapel steeple -

Rose the bubble (with the baby) slowly lifting up aloft.

There was such a flum-a-diddle (Mabel huddled in the middle),
Canon Dapple left the chapel, followed by the chapel choir.
And the treble singer, Abel, threw an apple core at Mabel,

As the baby in the bubble bobbled up a little higher.

Oh, they giggled and they goggled until all their brains were boggled,

As the baby in the bubble rose above the little town.

"With the problem let us grapple," murmured kindly Canon Dapple.

"And the problem we must grapple with is bringing Baby down."

"Now, let Mabel stand on Abel, who could stand in turn on Tybal,

Who could stand on Greville Gribble, who could stand upon the wall,

While the people from the shop'll stand to catch them if they topple,

Then perhaps they'll reach the bubble, saving Baby from a fall."

But Abel, though a treble, was a rascal and a rebel,

Fond of getting into trouble when he didn't have to sing.

Pushing quickly through the people, Abel clambered up the steeple

With nefarious intentions and a pebble in his sling!

Abel quietly aimed the pebble past the steeple of the chapel,
At the baby in the bubble wibble-wobbling way up there.
And the pebble burst the bubble! So the future seemed to fizzle
For the baby boy who grizzled as he tumbled through the air.

What a moment for a mother as her infant plunged above her!

There were groans and gasps and gargles from the horror-stricken crowd.

Sybil said, "Upon my honour, there's a baby who's a goner!"
And Chrysta hissed with emphasis, "It shouldn't be allowed!"

But Mabel, Tybal, Greville and the jogger (christened Neville)
Didn't quiver, didn't quaver, didn't drivel, shrivel, wilt.
But as one they made a swivel, and with action (firm but civil),
They divested Mrs Threeble of her pretty patchwork quilt.

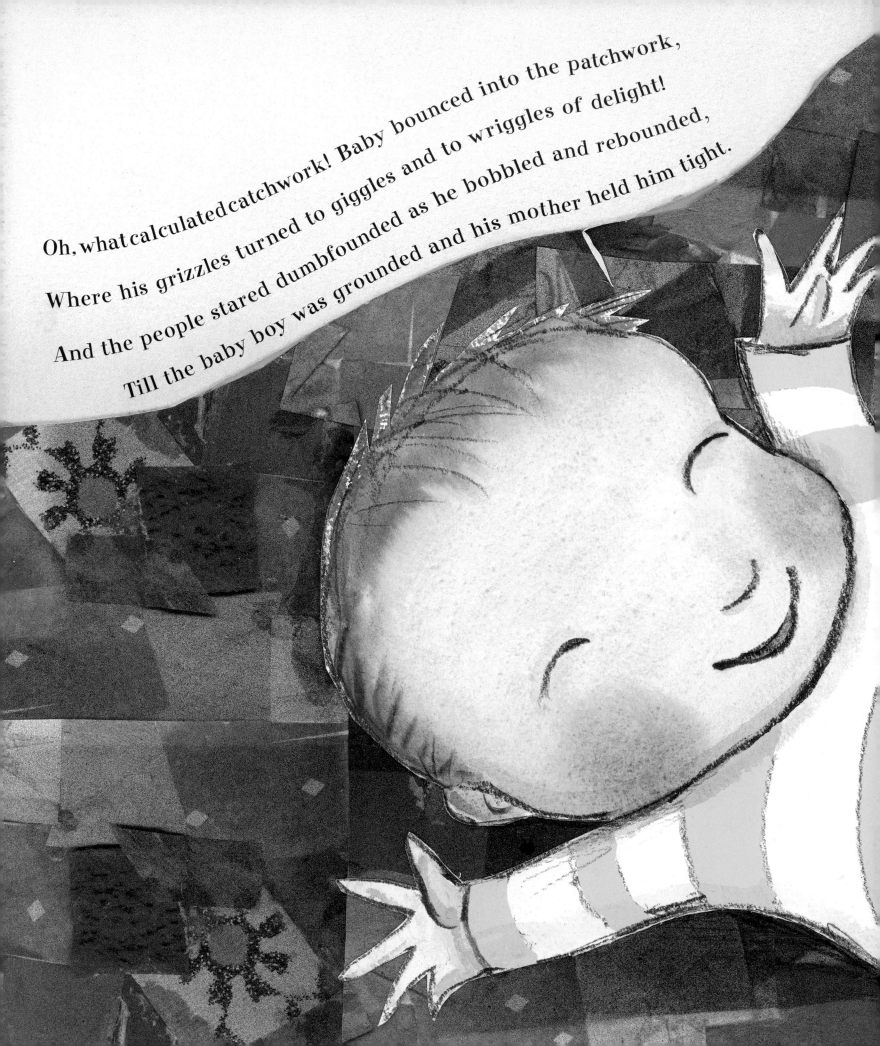

Oh, what calculated catchwork! Baby bounced into the patchwork,
Where his grizzles turned to giggles and to wriggles of delight!
And the people stared dumbfounded as he bobbled and rebounded,
Till the baby boy was grounded and his mother held him tight.

And the people there still prattle – there is lots of tittle-tattle –

For the glory in the story, young and old folk, gold and grey,

Of how wicked treble Abel tripled trouble with his pebble,

But how Mabel (and some others) saved her brother and the day.

MORE TITLES FROM FRANCES LINCOLN CHILDREN'S BOOKS

Down the Back of the Chair
Margaret Mahy
Illustrated by Polly Dunbar

When Dad loses his keys, toddler Mary suspects they are down the back of the chair.
Join in the fun as the family search and find everything from a bandicoot and a bumblebee to a string of pearls and a lion with curls. But will it be enough to save the family from rack and ruin?

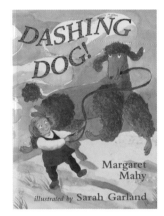

Dashing Dog!
Margaret Mahy
Illustrated by Sarah Garland

Follow the chaotic antics of the dashing dog and his family in a mad, dizzy and joyful walk along the beach. With Margaret Mahy's wildly funny sense of humour and Sarah Garland's exuberant illustrations, this is a picture book made in heaven!

Measuring Angels
Lesley Ely
Illustrated by Polly Dunbar

When two little girls are given a sunflower seed, they argue and the little plant grows very badly. "That sunflower is not happy," says the teacher. So the children decide to make an angel to help the plant grow. A friendship
develops between the two girls and, as they grow to like each other, the little plant grows bigger and bigger. . .

Frances Lincoln titles are available from all good bookshops.
You can also buy books and find out more about your favourite titles,
authors and illustrators on our website: www.franceslincoln.com